MYSTERY HIDEOUT

Other Apple Paperbacks you might enjoy:

The Power Twins
by Ken Follett

Fire on the Ridge
by John Wells

Radio Fifth Grade
by Gordon Korman

The Lemonade Trick
by Scott Corbett

Secret Agents Four
by Donald J. Sobol

KEN FOLLETT

Interior illustrations by Stephen Marchesi

SCHOLASTIC INC.
New York Toronto London Auckland Sydney

Previously published in England as *The Secret of Kellerman's Studio*, 1976.

ISBN 0-590-42506-4

12 11 10 9 8 7 6 5 4 3 4 5 6/9

Printed in the U.S.A. 40

First Scholastic printing, June 1991

To my favorite cousins,
Timothy and Rachel Dodge,
with love

CHAPTER ONE

Mick Williams pushed the last evening newspaper through a mailbox and jumped onto his bike. He pedaled fast back toward the paper shop. He always enjoyed this part of the job. The bag, which was so painfully heavy at the start of his route, now fluttered behind him, empty.

He turned a corner and rode across the road straight at the pavement. A split second before he hit the curb, he yanked at the handlebars to lift the front wheel off the ground. The bike rode smoothly onto the pavement. Mick jammed on the back brake and stopped beside the shop window with a neat back-wheel skid. It was a trick he had learned long ago.

He leaned the bike against the shop wall

and went in. As he opened the door he noticed a boy he did not know, standing with his hand on the saddle of a racer by the shop window. He hoped the stranger had been impressed with his riding.

Mr. Thorpe, the news dealer, said, "There's a new boy outside, Mick. Will you show him route seven?"

"Righto," Mick said. He got extra money each week for doing odd jobs like this. He knew every route in the shop, so if one of the boys did not turn up, Mick would do the route. If there was no extra work, he would sweep the shop out and then go home.

Mick tapped on the window and waved the new boy to come in. Mr. Thorpe called out, "Mick Williams will show you around, son."

Mick looked at the boy. He guessed they were about the same age, although the new boy was taller and bigger than Mick. He had short fair hair, and Mick noticed he was wearing a button-down shirt.

"What's your name?" Mick asked.

"Randall Izard," the boy said.

"Funny name."

"At my old school they called me Izzie," the boy said.

Mick took the boy's paper bag from him and laid it flat on the counter with the *News of*

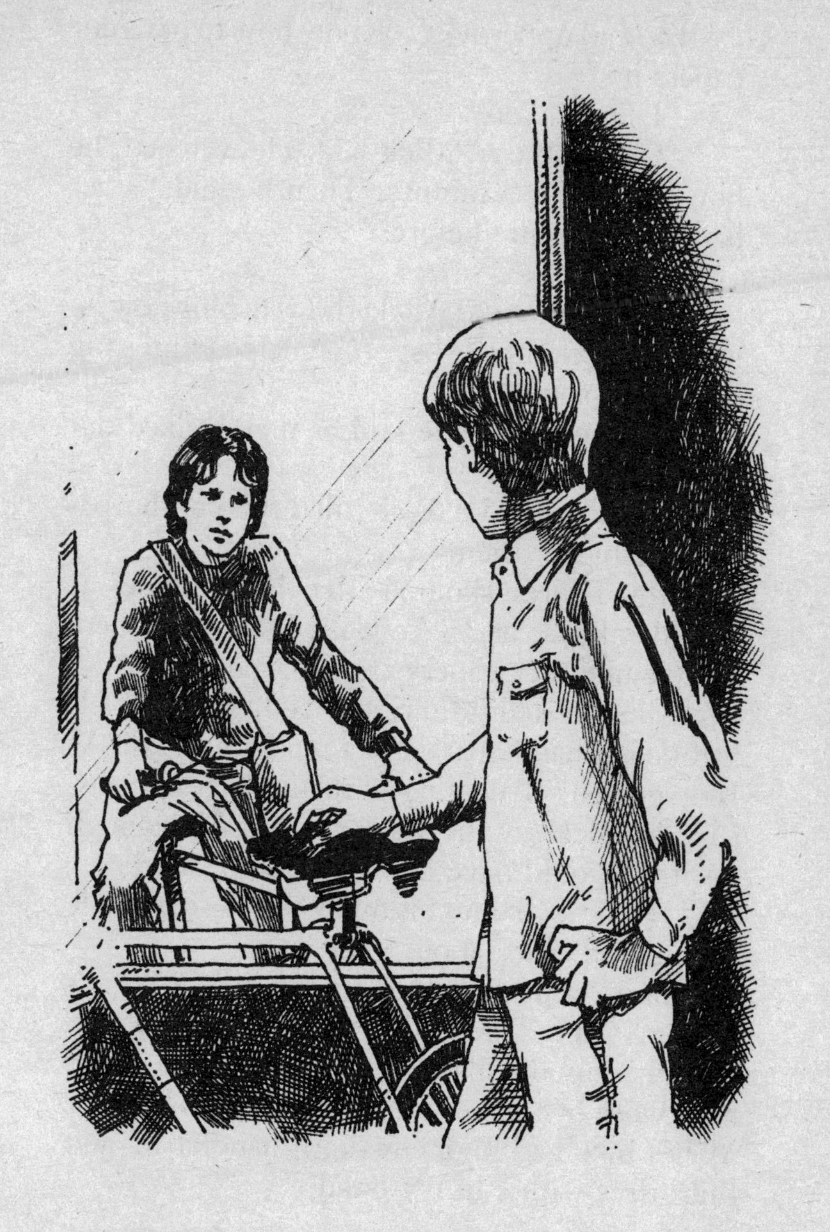

the World ad uppermost. "Know how to put your papers in?"

"I suppose so."

"Go on, then," Mick said. He watched the boy fumble for a minute. Then he said, "Ever had a paper route before?"

"No."

"I thought so." Mick showed him how to put the papers in the bag, then helped him sling it over his shoulder.

"It's heavy," Izzie said as they walked out of the shop.

Mick laughed. "Wait till Friday—the papers are bigger then."

Mr. Thorpe shouted after them: "Quick as you like, boys, or 35 Acacia will be round here complaining her papers are late again."

Mick looked admiringly at Izzie's bike. It had racing handlebars and a ten-speed gear. As Izzie got on, struggling with the bag of newspapers, Mick saw he was only just big enough for it. It would have been too big for Mick.

He jumped onto his own bike. As they rode off he said, "Pity about your bike."

Izzie went a bit red in the face. "What's wrong with it?" he asked.

"It's a good bike," Mick said. "But it makes hard work of a paper route. This sort is better." Mick's bike had high cow-horn handlebars and thick tires with a heavy tread.

"I didn't get it for a paper route," the boy muttered.

They turned into Acacia Avenue and Mick pointed out the first house. As they went along, he told Izzie which houses wanted the paper left on the doorstep, where it had to be pushed through the mailbox so it would not get wet if it rained, and where the people would not let him walk across the lawn and take a shortcut over the hedge.

Izzie said, "Was this your route before?"

"I've done them all one time or another," Mick said. He did not like the new boy much, he decided. Izzie had a posh voice. People who talked like that were usually snobby.

He studied Izzie's bike while he waited for him to come back down a long drive. The narrow-rimmed wheels had high-pressure tires with a racing tread. It must have been an expensive bike. Izzie must be quite rich, with his posh voice and his expensive bike. Mick wondered why he was doing a paper route.

Izzie came back through the gate. His bag was almost empty now. Mick said, "Who gave you the bike?"

"Birthday present from my father," Izzie replied. "Where did you get yours?"

"Stole it," Mick said, and rode on to the next house.

A couple of houses later he said, "What does your dad do for a living, then?"

"He makes films," Izzie said.

Mick was impressed. "What, cowboys and James Bond and all that stuff?"

"No. Television ads, mostly."

"Oh," Mick said. That was not nearly so interesting.

"What about yours?" Izzie asked.

"My what?"

"Father."

"I haven't got one," Mick said. Izzie frowned and opened his mouth to ask another question, but Mick said, "That's your last house. Go on."

As they rode back to the shop Mick asked, "What school do you go to, then?"

"Radley."

That was Mick's school. "I haven't seen you," he said.

"I only just started there," Izzie explained. "I used to go to boarding school."

At the shop, Mick did his back-wheel skid again while Izzie carefully parked his bicycle at the curb. They went inside.

Mr. Thorpe said to Izzie, "All right, son, see you at quarter past four tomorrow."

When he had gone Mr. Thorpe asked Mick, "How was he?"

"He'll do," Mick said. He picked up an evening paper from the counter and put a coin on the till.

Mr. Thorpe said, "Seems a nice boy."

Mick put the paper in his bag. "He's a bit snobby, but I think his family must have fallen on hard times."

"Oh, really?" said Mr. Thorpe, a little smile turning up the corners of his mouth.

"So long," said Mick, and went home.

Izzie rode home very fast, his head bent over the handlebars, changing swiftly through the gears. It's a great bike, whatever Mick Williams may say, he thought to himself. His old crock looks homemade, and it must weigh a ton.

Still, he had all evening to himself now. No school until tomorrow morning. He dreaded the thought of going to Radley. He had no friends there, although his mother said he would soon make some. Still, he wished he could go back to boarding school, where he had been on the soccer team. Changing schools was miserable.

To cheer himself up he thought about what he would do when he got home. Perhaps he would get the soldiers out. It was a long time since he had fought a battle.

He sprinted up the drive to his house and stopped with a skid on the gravel. It wasn't as good as Mick Williams's skid, but it would improve with practice.

His mother was in the kitchen, getting meat out of the freezer. They always used to have an au pair girl to help with the cooking and things, but not anymore.

"Hello, Randall. How did the paper route go?" his mother said.

"Fine," he said. He never told Mother his troubles these days. He reckoned she had enough to worry about, what with Father finding it difficult to get work because of the slump in the film industry. So he kept it all inside himself, and told her everything was just great.

"I'm going to get the army out," he told her.

"All right," she said. "Don't go on too long. Dinner is at seven, and you must have a bath beforehand."

Izzie hung up his parka in the downstairs closet and went up to the playroom. He decided to fight the battle of Dunkirk. He laid a piece of tape out on the carpet in the shape of the French coastline, and started arranging the German soldiers in their positions. Soon he was lost in the imaginary war.

Mick let himself in by the front door. He saw the landlord's wife lurking down the dim passageway. "It's only me, Mrs. Grewal," he called.

He went up the stairs. The Irish woman on the first floor was cooking her husband's

story hotel on the site of the disused Kellerman's Studio on Canal Street, West Hinchley."

Canal Street was Mick's address, and the old studio was right behind his house. It was in a huge building as big as a hospital, surrounded by barbed-wire fences and patrolled at night by men with dogs. The place had closed down a year ago, and now only an occasional van went in and out through the gate a few doors down from Mick's house.

Mick heard his mom come into the kitchen. She called: "Are you home, Mickey?"

"Yes," he called back.

She came into the room and sat down heavily in the old armchair. She unbuttoned her coat and lit a cigarette. Mick folded the paper up.

Mom said, "I don't know how you can watch television and read the paper at the same time."

Mick said, "It says in the paper there's going to be a hotel at the back. They must be going to pull the old studio down."

"What do you want for your tea?"

"I'll have a bacon sandwich."

Mom dumped her coat on the bed in the corner and went into the kitchen. Mick followed her. He watched her light the gas and get some bacon out of the cupboard.

"I don't suppose they'll want these old houses in front of their nice new hotel," he said.

"I don't know what they want a hotel here for anyway," Mom replied. "Who would want to stay in Canal Street for a holiday?"

Mick got out two plates and two knives. He thought for a minute and said, "I suppose, with the new road going through, it'll be handy for the airport."

Mom said nothing. She slapped two strips of bacon in the pan and plugged in the kettle for a cup of tea.

Mick said, "It would spoil a nice new hotel, though—to have these ugly houses all around it."

"You're old beyond your years," Mom sighed. "I keep forgetting you're almost a man. Sit down at the table now."

Mick looked curiously at his mother. She didn't seem to be talking sense. He waited for her to explain.

She made up the two sandwiches and sat down opposite him, dumping the plates on the plastic tablecloth.

Mick poured brown sauce into his and took a big bite, crunching the crisp bacon rind with his teeth.

"They're going to knock these houses down," Mom said. "They've bought the land from Mr. Grewal."

"They can't knock them down with people

in them," Mick said, his mouth full of bread and bacon.

"We've got to get out," she replied. "We've had notice to leave."

"Oh." Mick was not much bothered, but his mother seemed a bit upset. "We'll have to find another apartment, then."

She pushed her plate toward him. "Here, I don't want this." She got up to make the tea. "You don't understand," she said. "It's not so easy, finding another apartment." She poured her tea and came back to the table. She lit another cigarette. "You don't remember the last time. Dragging around the streets, landlords who said the apartment was taken as soon as they saw I had a child, agencies who laugh in your face when you tell them what you want."

She drank her tea and puffed at the cigarette. "I can't face it all again," she said. She got up and went into the other room.

Mick put down his sandwich. He had never seen his mother so upset. He had seen her angry, arguing with people, he had seen her cry over a sad movie on television, he had even seen her drunk. But this helpless sadness was new to him. It made him feel a bit choked up inside.

He got up and leaned on the doorpost, looking into the other room. Mom was sitting in the armchair, looking at the poster of Majorca on the opposite wall. There were tears in her eyes.

Mick said, “It’s the same for everyone else in the street.”

“The other women have husbands,” she said. “It’s different when there’s a man.”

“You’ve got me,” Mick said.

Mom smiled through her tears. “Yes, I’ve got you.”

“You don’t think I can do anything, do you?”

She shook her head slowly. “No, Mickey, I don’t think you can.”

Mick felt angry now. “You’ll see,” he said. He went out.

CHAPTER TWO

At school the next day Izzie saw Mick Williams, but they did not speak until after lunch. A game of soccer was organized in the playground, and Izzie asked if he could join in.

He was picked to play on the same side as Mick. They were both forwards. It took a few minutes for Izzie to get used to playing with a tennis ball.

They were standing together in the middle of the pitch when a wild kick came up from their own goalie and went out to the wing. Izzie dashed across to get it. When he looked around he saw that Mick had gone right upfield.

Two defenders rushed toward Izzie. He lifted the ball over their heads and it dropped right at Mick's feet. Mick stopped it, turned on one foot, and scored.

After that they worked together well, creating opportunities for each other. Mick was good at finding a space, and Izzie's passing was precise. They scored three more.

When the whistle blew for lessons and they crowded back into the school building, Mick put an arm on Izzie's shoulder. He turned to the others and said, "Didn't he do well?"

Izzie beamed with pleasure.

That evening Mick finished his paper route and went back to the shop. He saw that all the routes had gone out, so he picked up the broom and started to sweep the shop out. Izzie came in from his route while Mick was sweeping.

Mick said, "I might have to leave this job, Mr. Thorpe."

Mr. Thorpe looked up from his books and took off his glasses. "Why?" he said.

"I might be moving. They're going to knock our house down for a hotel. We've got to find somewhere else to live."

"I'm sorry to hear that," said Mr. Thorpe. "Won't you be able to find another place nearby?"

"My mom says it will be hard to find a place at all."

"I suppose it will," said Mr. Thorpe. "I

shall be sorry to lose you. Why would they build a hotel there, I wonder?"

"They're going to knock down Kellerman's Studio."

"I see." Mr. Thorpe put his glasses back on and returned to his books. Mick swept the dust out through the shop door and put the broom in the back room.

Izzie said, "My father used to work in Kellerman's Studio. Have you ever been in there?"

"Can't get in," Mick replied.

"I know a way," said Izzie.

Mr. Thorpe looked up from his books again. "If you lads are plotting mischief, do it outside the shop," he said. "I don't want to know about it."

The boys went outside to their bikes. "How can you get into the studio?" Mick asked. His curiosity was aroused now.

"You have to go across the canal and up a drain," Izzie said. "I'll show you, if you want."

"All right," said Mick excitedly. "Tomorrow?"

"Okay, then. I'll call for you. Where do you live?"

"Canal Street. Number 17."

"It's Saturday tomorrow. I'll come round in the morning. We'll have to wear old clothes in case we get dirty."

They got on their bikes and rode off in opposite directions.

Mick was sitting on the front steps, tying the laces of his sneakers, when Izzie arrived. He squinted into the sunshine and said, "Hi." Izzie was wearing jeans and a sweater with a hole in the sleeve.

Mick stood up and walked down the steps. Izzie said, "Where can I leave my bike? In the back garden?"

"That belongs to the landlord," Mick said. "You can put it down there." He pointed to a flight of steps which led down from the pavement to the basement door. There was a small concrete yard at the bottom, where the garbage cans were kept. Izzie got a padlock and chain out of his pocket, locked the front wheel of his bike to the frame so it could not be ridden away, and carried the bicycle down the steps.

"Want a hand?" Mick said.

"No thanks, it's very light," Izzie replied. He leaned the bike against a wall and came back up the steps. His nose wrinkled. "Stinks down there," he said.

The two boys walked down the street. They passed a break in the terraced houses, where the entrance to the old studio was. There was a high wire gate, with rolls of barbed wire above it. Behind that the rough road, with cracks and potholes, ran up between the houses, past a small hut, to the main entrance of the studio. The hut was used by the security men who guarded the place at night.

Fifty yards farther on the houses ended and the boys came to the canal bridge. They leaned over the parapet and looked down. Because it was summer, the canal was almost dry. A trickle of water flowed slowly down a narrow channel in the soft mud.

"I wonder why it dries up in summer?" Mick said.

Izzie said, "It's fed by a stream at one end, and runs into the Thames at the other. The stream dries up when there's no rain."

The canal bed was littered with junk. Mick could see an old bedstead, a car door, a few bottles, and a lot of unidentifiable garbage, all the same dirty gray color as the mud.

On their left, beside the last house on Canal Street, there was a high wall. But the opposite side of the canal had a low embankment. Izzie pointed to it. "We have to get onto the bank," he said.

Mick considered the problem. Where the bridge parapet ended, there was a high chicken-wire fence reaching down below the level of the pavement.

He pulled himself onto the parapet and stood up. Then he swung onto the back of the fence, pushing the toes of his sneakers into the holes in the wire. He climbed down as far as he could go, then jumped. It was a drop of about four feet from the bottom of the wire to the canal bank. Mick landed lightly, and shouted up: "It's dead easy."

In a moment Izzie was beside him on the embankment. They walked along slowly, picking their way through the brambles and avoiding the clumps of nettles.

"I bet there's rats here," Mick said.

"How do you know?" Izzie asked skeptically.

"Always are, near water."

At one point the whole width of the bank was taken up by an old car. It was rusting and had no doors or wheels.

"I wonder how that got here?" Izzie said with a frown. Next to the canal was a railway line, and after that a factory. There seemed no way the car could have been brought to the spot.

They followed the embankment around a slight curve until they were out of sight of the bridge and near the back of the studio. Then Izzie pointed across the canal and said, "There it is."

Mick followed the direction of his finger and saw a large pipe coming out of the opposite bank. In winter, the pipe would be covered by the water, he realized.

Izzie said, "That pipe leads right inside the studio."

Mick looked around him. In the long grass he found a rotten old scaffolding plank. When he picked it up, all sorts of little insects scurried out from underneath it.

"This will help us get across the canal," he said.

He stood on the edge of the bank, holding the plank upright in front of him. He shifted sideways until he was right opposite the pipe. Then he let the plank fall.

It made a little squishy sound as it hit the mud. "Good idea!" Izzie said. They could now walk across without getting their feet muddy.

Izzie reached under his sweater and took a pencil flashlight from his T-shirt pocket. "I'd better go first," he said.

He put the flashlight between his teeth and lowered himself over the edge onto the plank. It sank slightly into the mud as he trod carefully across it. At the other side, he switched on his flashlight and put it back in his mouth, with the beam pointing outward. Then he put his head and shoulders into the pipe. Mick saw that the pipe was plenty big enough for him, although it would have been too small for a grown-up.

"Come on," Izzie shouted back over his shoulder. Mick dropped down onto the plank and followed in Izzie's footsteps.

The inside of the pipe had a musty smell as he put his head in. But as he crawled along behind Izzie, he realized it was fairly dry. Obviously it had not been used for a long time.

The light from the opening behind them petered out after a few feet, and only the slim beam of Izzie's flashlight showed the way.

The air got colder, and the concrete under Mick's hands began to feel wet. Suddenly he remembered what he had said to Izzie about rats. He felt a bit scared. Rats attack when they get cornered, he knew.

They were going slightly uphill. Eventually Izzie shined his flashlight upward and said, "Here we are."

Mick peered over his shoulder. The beam of the light showed an upward tunnel. Izzie said, "There's a manhole at the top. I'll have to stand on your shoulders." He stood up, the top of his body hidden in the upper pipe.

Mick crawled between his legs and knelt upright. He guided Izzie's feet onto his shoulders and struggled to stand. He looked up.

Izzie was feeling around a metal plate—the manhole cover, Mick guessed. "Get ready to take the strain," Izzie called. He put his hands flat against the plate and pushed. Mick braced himself against the sides of the pipe. Suddenly the pressure lifted. "Done it!" Izzie said excitedly.

His feet left Mick's shoulders as he pulled

himself up out of the manhole. Then he reached back inside. "I'll pull you," he said. Mick took his hand.

He put his feet against one side of the pipe and his back against the other. With Izzie's help he shuffled up the pipe in that way until he could reach the rim of the manhole with his hands. Then he heaved himself out.

They stood in the darkness, peering around as Izzie's flashlight wandered over the walls. They were in a kind of storeroom, with lockers all along the sides. Izzie said, "I think this manhole must have been outside originally, then they built this part as an extension to the main building."

The flashlight lit up a door, and Izzie walked over and opened it. The boys went through into a corridor. There was a thick film of dust everywhere and cobwebs around the doorway.

"This corridor runs all the way around the building," Izzie said. He was whispering, although there was no reason to. "On the outside are the offices, and the studios are on the inside. So they have no windows."

He crossed the corridor and shined the flashlight above a door. A sign said: "Studio B. Positively no entry when red light on." He opened the door and went in. Mick followed him.

Izzie found a light switch and turned it on. Suddenly Mick found himself in the Wild West.

Right in front of him was a set of doors with a painted wooden sign saying "Saloon." Behind that was a long bar, and on it a bottle and some glasses. The floor looked like wood, but Mick could see that the stained planks had just been painted onto the linoleum. Half a dozen wooden tables, with rickety-looking chairs, stood on the other side of the saloon.

"Fantastic!" Mick breathed. Putting on a swagger, he pushed his way through the doors, walked up to the bar, and banged on it. "Whiskey," he said in his best cowboy accent.

"Good, isn't it?" Izzie said. He walked across the saloon to where there should have been a back wall. Instead there was a row of quite modern cupboards. Izzie opened one and took out a Stetson.

He put it on his head and pulled the string tight. It was much too big for him, but perched on the back of his head it just about stayed on.

Mick opened another cupboard and gave a long whistle. "Guns!" he said. He took one out. It was surprisingly big and heavy, and slightly oily. He found a holster and belt in another cupboard, and strapped them on. Izzie did the same.

They looked at themselves in a big mirror

on the wall. Now they both wore cowboy hats, gun belts, and holsters. They rummaged in the cupboard and found boots with spurs on.

Mick sat on a chair in the saloon, tilted it, and stuck his boots on the table. He closed one eye. "Muh name's Deadeye Dick," he muttered. "Don't nobody cross me—an' live, thet is."

Izzie went out of the saloon, then came slouching back through the doors. "Hey, son," he called to an imaginary boy. "Take care o' muh horse." He went up to the bar and pretended to pour from the bottle.

"Hey, barman. Ah'm a stranger in these parts. Lookin' fer a character name o' Dick Bartlett. Leastways, that's his real name. Ah'm figgerin' on shootin' it out with thet old rattlesnake. Y'know him?"

Mick tilted his hat farther down over his eyes. "You talkin' about me, mister?" he drawled.

Izzie turned around slowly. "Go fer your gun, Deadeye," he said.

Mick let his chair crash to the floor. Izzie's hand went to his holster. Mick drew first and fired. There was a terrific bang, and the bottle on the bar shattered. Izzie gave a terrified yell.

The two boys looked at one another. Mick's face was deathly pale. "I didn't think there would be real bullets in it," he said.

"Blimey," Izzie whispered. He looked at

the pieces of broken glass on the floor and the yellow liquid running over the bar. "Blimey," he said again.

Then, in the silence after the bang, they both heard a noise. "Listen!" Izzie said.

"Ssh!" Mick hissed.

The noise grew louder. It was a truck coming up the drive to the studio.

"Quick!" Mick said. The two of them began taking off their cowboy clothes. They heaved off the boots and put their own shoes on. Then they dumped the hats, guns and belts on the floor. It seemed to take ages.

They hurried over to the door. Izzie switched out the light and opened the door. The corridor was pitch dark.

They took one step forward. Suddenly a light appeared, far down the corridor, on their right. It jerked around, as if it came from a flashlight someone was carrying. The boys froze.

Another light appeared, and they heard a voice. It seemed to break the spell. They both dived back into Studio B. Izzie shut the door quietly.

They held their breath as the voices came nearer. Mick whispered, "What do we do if they come in here?"

"Give ourselves up," Izzie replied softly.

"We can't—"

"Hush!"

The footsteps came up to the door. A voice said, ". . . thought the old fool was thinking of giving it a try, so I . . ." The footsteps started to fade again as the men passed the door.

Mick let his breath out in a long sigh. Suddenly there was light. Izzie gasped. Mick looked up. The light came from the next studio. There was only a partition between the two studios, and there was a big gap between the top of the partition and the high roof of the building. The men had gone into the next studio and switched on the lights.

Izzie opened the door to the corridor. Suddenly the other door, across the room, which led to the next studio, swung open. Light poured through. A man said, "Might have left it in here somewhere."

The two boys were out of their door in no time. They dashed across the corridor and into the storeroom. Izzie flashed his light around the floor until it rested on the manhole. He lowered himself into it and dropped. Mick followed.

They scuttled down the pipe, grazing their hands and knees in their hurry. Before long there was daylight ahead.

Izzie fell straight out of the pipe into the canal mud. Mick fell on top of him.

Their plank had sunk below the surface.

They waded through the slime and hauled themselves up on the bank.

Breathless, but safe, they sat on the bank and looked at each other. They were both covered with mud.

Relief flooded through them and they burst out laughing.

▶ 30

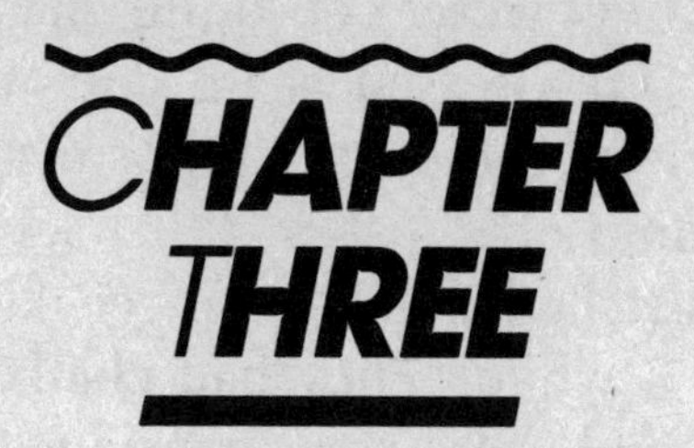

CHAPTER THREE

Luckily, Mick's mom was out when he got home. He took off his muddy trousers and shirt and washed them in the kitchen sink. Then he spread them on the floor in front of the electric heater to dry.

He washed the mud out of his long brown hair in the bathroom down the hall—he and his mom shared it with the Irish couple. He had no coins for the gas heater, so he used cold water.

He sat in front of the heater waiting for his hair and clothes to dry. He could have put on his other trousers, but he was supposed to save them for best until this pair wore out. It was all very well for Izzie, he thought. He obviously had lots of trousers. Mick had only two pairs.

He soon got tired of waiting. He felt the

clothes. They were not quite dry, but they would do. He dressed again and went downstairs to sit on the steps. The sunshine would take the damp off.

He watched some younger kids playing cricket for a while. They had chalked a wicket on a wall, and there were continual arguments as to whether the ball hit the stumps or not.

A dirty white Ford drew up at the curb, a little way down the road, and two men got out. Mick looked at them curiously. They were strangers. One was a youngish chap in a smart suit. The older man wore a hat and carried a camera.

They stood by their car for a couple of minutes. Mrs. Briggs, the woman in the house next to the studio entrance, came along carrying two bags of groceries. The men stopped her.

Mick sauntered down the steps and along the pavement. He leaned against the railings where he could hear the conversation.

The young man said to Mrs. Briggs, "We're from the *Hinchley News*. My name's Nigel Parsons, and this is our photographer Mr. Cotton."

"Oh, yes?" said Mrs. Briggs. She put her bags down and eyed the men suspiciously.

Nigel Parsons continued: "We've come to find out what the people on Canal Street think about the plan to build a hotel on the site of Kellerman's Studio."

"It's a scandal," said Mrs. Briggs.

"Why do you say that?" the reporter asked her. Old Mrs. Arkwright opened her door then, pretending to be shaking out a duster, although really she just wanted to know what was going on.

Mrs. Briggs called out, "Come out here a minute, Mrs. Arkwright. Gentlemen from the papers, talking about Kellerman's Studio."

"Oh, yes," said Mrs. Arkwright eagerly. She came down her steps. "You listen to me, young man," she said, wagging her finger at the reporter. "We've all had notice to leave. Every one of us."

Mrs. Briggs interrupted: "See, the studio owns nearly all the houses. There was one or two private landlords, but now they've sold out to the people who want to build this here hotel."

Mick walked away then, back to his own steps. He had forgotten all about the plans to knock the houses down—and his promise to his mom that he would do something about it.

He watched the men from the *Hinchley News.* A small crowd gathered around them. Nigel Parsons had his notebook out, writing down what the women were saying.

What can I do? Mick thought. The photographer was moving around the group now, taking pictures of the women as they talked to the reporter. Mick could not see that pictures in the paper would do any good. But what would?

Al Capone would have sent a couple of the boys around to put the pressure on, Mick thought. That was a useless idea. He wondered about the man who had bought the studio and all the houses. Maybe he had a weak spot, like Achilles' heel.

I could try to find out something about the man who bought the place, Mick thought. At least it would be a start. He went back to where the crowd was.

Mrs. Briggs was saying, "Mind you, I've complained about the studio since it's been shut. There's a truck goes roaring up that drive, hooting its horn—in the middle of the night sometimes. I've written it down, every time it's done it—the date and the time. I can tell you—"

Mick said, "Mr. Parsons?" in a loud voice.

The reporter turned around. He looked happy at the interruption. "Yes, son?" he said.

"Do you know who has bought all this?"

"Yes. It's a property company called Hinchley Developments."

"Thanks." Mick walked away again. That was not much use.

He saw his mom coming down the road with the groceries and went in for his dinner.

Izzie and his father drove to Canal Street on Sunday morning. Izzie pointed out Mick's house, and his father parked outside.

The front door was open, and they walked in. An Indian lady at the back of the hall said, "Yes?"

"I'm looking for Mrs. Williams," said Mr. Izard.

"Top floor," the woman told him, and disappeared. Izzie and his father went up the stairs.

At the top they came to a brown paneled door. "I suppose this is it," said Mr. Izard.

He knocked on the door with his knuckles. After a moment, a woman in a faded pink housecoat came to the door. Izzie thought how much younger than his own mother she looked. Her hair was untidy, and she had no stockings on, but she might be quite pretty if she was dressed up, he thought.

"Mrs. Williams?" said Mr. Izard.

"Yes."

Mick's mother looked puzzled. She looked down at Izzie for a moment, then said, "Oh, you must be Izzie."

Izzie said, "That's what they all call me, Father."

"Well, you'd better come in," said Mrs. Williams.

"I'm afraid the place isn't very tidy," she said as she led them through the kitchen. "Sunday is my day for getting up late."

"I hope we haven't spoiled your sleep," Mr. Izard said.

Mick was lying on the floor watching Tarzan on TV. "Hello, Izzie," he said in a surprised tone. His mother switched the television off.

Izzie looked around him, puzzled. He couldn't tell whether this was the bedroom or the living room. Then he realized it was both.

They all sat down. Izzie's father said, "Randall told me you had notice to leave because of the hotel plan."

"That's right."

"You see, I've got an interest in preventing this hotel going up, too. There's a group of us—various people in the film industry—trying to get Kellerman's Studio going again. We've made some progress, although we need to raise a lot more money. But if this company gets planning permission for a hotel, the value of the site will soar. Then we will never be able to afford it."

Mick's mom said, "Is there any way of stopping it?"

"Yes. The council has to give them planning permission. We could try to persuade them to refuse. If all the residents around here got together with the film people, we might stand a chance."

Mick's mom lit a cigarette. "If I know anything, money talks louder than people when it comes to things like this," she said.

"Perhaps you're right," said Mr. Izard. "But it's worth a try. I was wondering whether you might form a committee of the residents, or get a petition up, perhaps. Then you could get hold of your ward councilors and tell them to oppose the plan."

Mrs. Williams blew out a cloud of smoke. "I'm not much of a one for committees and councilors," she said. "But I might see if anyone will sign a petition. I suppose it's worth a try, if it costs nothing."

"Good," said Mr. Izard. "I'm sure you'll find your neighbors will all rally round once someone takes the initiative." He stood up. "If there's anything I can do, at all, just let me know."

"Would you like a cup of tea?" Mrs. Williams asked.

"That's very nice of you, but we have to get back."

Mrs. Williams saw them out. Mick called, "See you tomorrow, Izzie."

"Righto," Izzie said.

As he and his father got into the car, Izzie said, "Mick's mother's nice."

"Yes," his father said quietly. "But what a dump they live in."

"Why do they want to stay there, then?"

His father looked at him. "It's their home, Randall."

Mick spent all Monday trying to figure out what he could do about the hotel plan. His teacher accused him of daydreaming, but he ignored her. He had more important things on his mind than coffee plantations in Kenya.

He didn't think Mr. Izard's schemes would come to anything. Petitions and committees were about as useless as pictures in the local paper, he reckoned.

But when he swept out the paper shop at the end of the day, he still had not come up with anything. Izzie stood waiting for him to finish.

Mick said, "Your dad's got long hair, for a dad."

"Lots of film people have long hair," Izzie said.

"Why?"

"Dunno."

Mr. Thorpe said, "Hurry up, Mickey. I want to close soon. I've got to address the Chamber of Commerce tonight."

"What's the Chamber of Commerce?" Mick said.

"Oh, all the businesspeople in town get together every so often."

Mick stood looking at Mr. Thorpe for a minute. He had an idea.

"Hurry up then," Mr. Thorpe said.

Mick swept the dust out of the front door and put the broom away. He and Izzie left the shop.

"Have you got a phone at your house?" Mick asked Izzie.

"Yes."

"Listen. I've got an idea. Will your mom let me call someone up?"

"She won't have to know," Izzie replied. "You can call from the upstairs phone."

"Great." They jumped on the bikes and pedaled off to Izzie's house.

On the way they stopped at a phone booth. Mick went in and looked up Hinchley Developments in the directory. He memorized the number.

When they went into Izzie's house, his mother was in the drawing room. Izzie took Mick in and introduced him. Mrs. Izard shook his hand. Izzie said, "I'm going to show Mick the trains."

"All right," his mother said.

The boys went upstairs to Izzie's playroom. Izzie looked at his watch. "You can make the phone call at quarter to six," he said. "She always watches the news then. You'll be sure she won't come upstairs."

They played with Izzie's train set for a while. It was a big electric one, laid out on a board. It had three trains, with stations, tunnels, junctions and sidings. Mick found it so interesting he was almost sorry when Izzie said, "Right. It's time."

They went into the master bedroom and Mick dialed the number he had memorized. It rang for a long time. Izzie said, "They may have gone home by now."

Then a voice answered: "Hinchley Developments, can I help you?"

Mick put on his best voice. "I'm sorry to trouble you," he said. "I'm doing a school project on the Hinchley Chamber of Commerce. Could you tell me the name of the boss of your company?"

"Certainly," said the woman on the other end of the line. "His name is Mr. Norton Wheeler. He's a very prominent businessman in Hinchley. I'm sure you'll want to mention him in your project."

"Norton Wheeler. Thank you very much," Mick said.

"A pleasure. If there's anything else I can do, please call again."

Mick said goodbye and hung up. Izzie said, "Terrific! That was clever!"

Mick was pleased with himself. "Now we know who it is that wants to knock my house down," he said. "Next thing is to find out all about him."

They went back into the playroom. Izzie said, "How do we find out about him, then?"

Mick frowned. "I'll have to think about it,"

he said. His jubilation began to fade. He picked up a boxcar and turned it over in his hands.

"I know what a spy would do," Izzie said.

"What?"

"Set a watch on his house."

Mick considered the idea. "It's better than nothing," he said. "We might pick up some clues. But first we need to find out where he lives."

"The phone book," Izzie said.

"Yes. We'll go back to the phone booth. We don't want your mother to get curious."

They switched off the train set and went out of the house. As they cycled down the road, Izzie said, "Course, he might be unlisted."

"What does that mean?" Mick asked.

"Not in the phone book."

"Why would he have a phone and not put the number in the phone book?"

"To stop every Tom, Dick, and Harry calling him up."

"He might as well not have a phone," said Mick. Some of the things grown-ups do just don't make sense, he thought to himself.

They stopped at a phone booth. They got off the bikes and went in. As they picked up the directory, Mick said under his breath, "You'd better be in here, Mr. Wheeler."

There were dozens of Wheelers. Mick ran

his fingers down the list, but none of the listings said Norton.

"Oh, blast," Mick said despairingly.

"Hold on, we're not defeated yet," Izzie said. "How many N. Wheelers are there?"

Mick counted. "Six."

"Right. Any in Hinchley?"

Mick looked at the addresses. Izzie peered over his shoulder. "There!" Izzie shouted. The address said 49 Clifton Drive. The name was Wheeler, N. After the name were the letters F.R.C.S

"What does F.R.C.S. mean?" Mick wondered.

"Wait a minute," Izzie said. He scratched his head. "Fellow of the Royal College of . . . Surgeons!" he announced triumphantly. Then his face fell. "That means he's a doctor," he said.

"So that's not Norton Wheeler," Mick said. "Is there another N. Wheeler in Hinchley?"

They looked again. The last name in the Ns was at 3 King Edward Avenue, Hinchley.

"I reckon that's him," Izzie said.

"How can we make sure?" asked Mick.

Izzie thought for a minute. "Phone the number," he said.

"We can't use your mother's phone again," said Mick. He felt in his pockets. "And I haven't got any money."

Izzie emptied his jacket pockets. He pulled out a handkerchief, a piece of string, two peppermints, a box of matches, a screwdriver—and a ten-pence coin.

He picked up the receiver and dialed the number. He held the headset away from his ear so that Mick could listen in.

A woman answered. "Hello?" she said.

Izzie pushed the coin into the slot, then put his hand over the mouthpiece. "What do I say?" he whispered.

Mick took the receiver from him. Izzie knew a lot of things, he thought, but at times he was plain stupid.

"Is Mr. Norton Wheeler at home, please?" Mick asked.

"No, he's not here yet," the woman said. "Can I help you?"

Mick put the phone down. "It is the right one," he said.

"We're in luck," Izzie said.

"About time we had some," Mick replied.

They met at the shop the next day, when they had finished their paper routes. They borrowed a street map from behind the counter and looked up King Edward Avenue. It was just over a mile away.

They made plans before they set out. Izzie

said what they were doing was called surveillance, and secret agents did it all the time. "It can get very boring," he said. Mick found it all rather exciting.

King Edward Avenue was a quiet road with trees along the curbs. All the houses were large and expensive-looking. Wheeler's house had a long front garden with lots of bushes and a high double garage at the side.

Mick and Izzie rode straight past it the first time. They went around a few more streets to see whether there was a back entrance, but they did not find one.

They parked the bikes a couple of houses away from No. 3. Then, in order not to look suspicious, they started to kick a tennis ball against the curb.

Nothing happened for about half an hour. Mick was beginning to see what Izzie meant about surveillance being boring, when a blue Jaguar swept past them and into the driveway of No. 3. Mick caught a glimpse of a dark-haired man behind the wheel.

They stopped the game. "I must get a closer look at him," Mick said.

"You don't even know that's him," Izzie pointed out.

"I'll find out," Mick said. He bounced the tennis ball and kicked it over the wall into the garden. Then he ran up the driveway.

The dark-haired man was just getting out of the car. Mick called, "Can I get my ball, Mr. Wheeler?"

The man frowned. "All right, but take it somewhere else and play," he said.

"Thanks." Mick dived into the bushes, located the tennis ball, and walked back down the driveway. At the gate he turned and looked at the car's license plate. He memorized it, then went back to Izzie.

"Was it him?" Izzie asked.

"Must be. I called him Mr. Wheeler, and he didn't seem surprised."

"Did you get a good look at him?"

"Yes."

They resumed their game. Eventually Izzie said, "Well, what else do we want to find out?"

"We should look for clues—anything that tells us anything about him. Know your enemy, they say."

"Well, we're not finding out much, just playing outside his house."

"You said it might be boring," Mick replied. "Let's hang on."

A few minutes later they heard the car start up again. They watched it come out of the driveway and roar off down the road. This time there was a woman in the passenger seat.

"Must be his wife," Mick said.

Izzie looked at his watch. "It's six-thirty—perhaps they're going out to dinner."

"So—we can have a closer look at the house."

Izzie looked startled. "A bit risky, that," he said. "You don't know whether there's anyone else there. What's more, we've done nothing wrong so far. But breaking into a house is against the law."

"We should look around, anyway," Mick persisted. "Otherwise, we've got nothing for our trouble."

Izzie bounced the tennis ball against the wall and caught it. "I think this has been a bit of a waste of time anyway," he said.

"You don't have to come. Tell you what—you keep watch outside. If anyone comes, give three rings on your bicycle bell."

"All right," Izzie said reluctantly.

Mick padded softly up the driveway, his sneakers making no noise on the pavement. He suspected Izzie might be right about this being a waste of time, but he was determined to find some clues.

He kept close to the bushes, ready to duck behind the foliage if need be. But he got to the top of the driveway undisturbed.

He stood behind a tree and looked at the house. There was a front porch, and an alley up the side of the house. Next to the alley were the garages. One of the garage doors was open a little.

He wondered whether to try to get into the house. But the open garage door indicated that there might still be someone at home. He decided to look in the garage first.

He ran silently across the drive and slipped through the narrow opening into the garage. It had a side window, so he could see quite well. He looked around him.

It was a very ordinary garage. There was an electric lawn mower in a corner and some tools in a rack on the wall. A few cans of paint were stacked at the back.

Mick looked at the floor. It had patches of oil.

No clues.

Mick was about to leave when he saw something out of the corner of his eye. He bent down and picked up a folded piece of paper from the floor. Next to it was a small, fine brush, like a paintbrush. He examined them.

He heard a sharp "ping! ping! ping!" It was Izzie's bell. Someone was coming.

He looked out through the door and saw the blue Jaguar coming up the driveway. He looked around him quickly. The garage had a back door. But if he went out that way he could get trapped in the garden.

Would Wheeler put his car in the garage? Mick heard it come to a stop in the driveway. A door opened, and footsteps approached. Mick made a quick decision. He slipped out through the back door and closed it quietly.

He stood listening, his heart pounding loudly. Izzie had said he would be breaking the law.

He heard the door slide back on its squeaky casters, then the car was driven in. The engine died and the car door slammed. Then the garage doors were closed. Mick breathed a sigh of relief.

Suddenly the handle of the back door turned. Wheeler was coming out the back way—he must have closed the front door from the inside. Mick dived behind a garbage can. He heard a key turn in the lock, then footsteps going away.

He risked a peep over the top of the garbage can. Wheeler was just going in through the kitchen door.

Mick waited for him to disappear. Then he threw caution to the winds and ran as fast as he could down the alley, down the driveway, and out into the road.

"Let's go!" he shouted to Izzie. They jumped on their bikes and sped away.

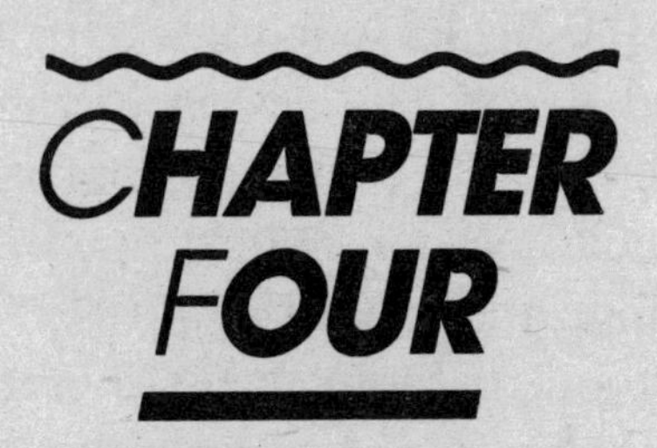

CHAPTER FOUR

Mrs. Briggs came round to Mick's apartment on Thursday afternoon with a copy of the weekly *Hinchley News*. Her picture was on page three. It showed her waving her arms about in front of her house. The report, by Nigel Parsons, was about the proposed demolition of the houses on Canal Street.

Mick's mom said, "It's a good picture, Mrs. Briggs." Mick looked at it. The woman looked terrible, with her mouth open wide and her hair all over the place.

"Well, I want to sign your petition," Mrs. Briggs said.

Mick's mom got a piece of paper out of the sideboard drawer and found a pen. Mrs. Briggs wrote her name on the bottom. "I see most have signed," she said.

"What does the paper say?" Mrs. Williams asked.

"It doesn't say anything about these trucks that keep coming up the driveway to the studio. Anyway, as I told that reporter, I've made a list of the dates and times they come. I've brought it for you to put in with your petition."

Mick looked up from the paper. "I don't see what that's got to do with it," he said.

"Shush, Mickey," his mother said. "Don't be so fresh." She took the two pieces of paper from Mrs. Briggs. "Thank you very much, dear," she said.

Mick returned to the newspaper. As his mom chatted with Mrs. Briggs, he read a report about the Disguise Gang. They had raided a post office last Saturday and got away with over a thousand pounds. It was the usual method: three or four of them went in and pretended to be customers, then waited for their opportunity to get behind the counter and rob the cash drawers.

They were still being very clever. They never left fingerprints, they used a stolen car for the getaway, and the police never found any clues. There was a picture of Detective-Inspector Peters looking baffled. Mick laughed.

Still, detecting wasn't so easy, he thought. He had gotten nowhere with Mr. Norton

Wheeler. The clues he and Izzie had picked up meant nothing. The piece of paper he had picked up on the garage floor turned out to be an ordinary bank deposit slip, the sort you fill in when you put money into your account, Izzie had said. The brush was just a brush. Mick had given up detecting for a while, until he could think of a new plan.

Mrs. Briggs said, "I must be on my way."

"Give the newspaper back to Mrs. Briggs, Mickey," Mom said.

Mick said, "Could I keep this page, please? I want to cut out the bit about the Disguise Gang."

"All right," she replied. Mick took out the sheet and gave the rest to Mrs. Briggs. The report had a roundup of all the Disguise Gang raids over the past few weeks. Mick decided he would make a Disguise Gang scrapbook, cutting out all the reports about them. Then, if they ever got caught, he could put their pictures in.

Izzie came in as Mrs. Briggs went out. From the kitchen Mick's mom called, "Are you going out, Mickey? Izzie's here."

Mick left the sheet of newspaper on the floor and went out. It was a mild summer evening, with several hours of light left. As the boys walked down the steet Mick said, "What are you going to be when you leave school?"

"A film director, I expect," Izzie replied. "You?"

"I'm going to be a villain," Mick said.

Izzie laughed. "Don't be crazy," he said.

"What's crazy about it? I'll be like the Disguise Gang—too clever for the police."

"My father says there are easier ways to make money than thieving," Izzie replied.

They came to the canal bridge. "Let's go in the studio again," Izzie said. Mick could think of nothing better to do, so he agreed.

They clambered down the wire fence and onto the canal bank, then made their way along to the pipe. Izzie said, "Did you really steal your bike?"

"Yeah," Mick said. "It was in the backyard of one of the shops. It was all rusty. I painted it up, got new wheels from the scrap yard round the corner, and bought the handlebars."

"That's not really stealing, though, is it?"

"Dunno."

This time there was no handy plank to help them across the canal. They found a couple of tires and a cushion from an armchair in the rubbish on the bank, and threw them into the canal to make a stepping-stone path across.

The drain did not seem so long now. Mick was surprised when Izzie stopped and shined his flashlight up into the manhole. They climbed up by the same method they had used the first time, and in a minute they were standing inside the storeroom again.

"We'll go into some of the other studios this time," Izzie said. He led the way across the corridor and into Studio C, the one the men had come into. "Keep your ears open for the sound of a truck," Izzie said.

When he switched the light on, Mick saw that this studio had been used to make a film about the Navy. One corner was done out as the bridge of a battleship, with dials, speaking tubes and assorted instruments. There was a pair of binoculars, which Mick looked through. They had no glass in them.

There was a piece of painted scenery up against one wall. It just showed a stretch of sea. Next to it was a cardboard cabin wall, with portholes painted on.

"Look at this!" Izzie said. "A film camera."

Mick walked over to it. "Does it work, do you think?" he said.

Izzie fiddled with it for a minute. "It's an old one," he said finally. "I expect that's why it's been left here to rust."

Mick left Izzie to play with the camera and went over to a ladder which reached up into the roof.

"What do you think this is for?" he asked Izzie.

"Getting up to fix the lights," Izzie replied.

Mick started up the ladder. It went quite high. At the top was a sort of platform. From there Mick could see the whole of Studio C laid out like a picture. Izzie looked very small. He could also see dimly into the other studios around, by reflected light.

"This is good," he called. "Come on up."

Izzie left the camera and came up the ladder. He lay beside Mick on the platform, looking down.

They both saw the studio door swing slowly open.

A man walked in. From their position right above him, all the boys could see was a bald spot on top of his head. They both held their breath.

The man said, "Which of you bright sparks left the light on here?"

Two more men followed him in. One of them carried a small suitcase. He put the case down and said, "Must have been me."

The man with the bald spot seemed to be satisfied with that. He gave a grunt and took his coat off. Mick and Izzie breathed again.

Mick put his mouth right next to Izzie's ear and whispered, "If we keep dead still, they may not notice us." Izzie nodded.

The three men took off their clothes and then washed their faces in the basin beside the

ladder. They dressed again, and opened the suitcase. It was full of money.

Izzie whispered to Mick, "They must be actors. They must have been out filming somewhere and come back to change."

The man with the bald spot said, "No time to bother with this now. We'll sort it out later. It's all mixed notes and coins." He closed the case again. The men left the studio.

Mick and Izzie stayed where they were, listening. Suddenly the door opened again, and the bald man came in and switched off the light. "Done it again, you twit," he said.

When he had gone, the boys waited until they heard the sound of a car start up and drive away. Only then did Izzie switch on his flashlight and start down the ladder.

Mick said, "This is getting a bit dangerous. They only had to look up to see us."

They found their way back to the storeroom by flashlight and got back into the drain. Their path was still intact when they reached the canal, and they got back across without having to dip their feet in the mud.

As they walked along the embankment, Izzie said, "I don't really understand it."

"What?"

"What they were doing there. I mean, if they were making a film, where were the director, the camera crew, the wardrobe and makeup people, and all the rest? Besides, the studio is supposed to be closed."

"Perhaps they're just allowed to use it occasionally," Mick suggested.

"Must be," said Izzie.

It was getting dark now, so Izzie unlocked his bike and rode off home. Mick went up to his apartment.

His mother was watching television. "It's time you learned to clean up after yourself," she said. "Put that piece of paper away."

Mick picked up his page from the *Hinchley News*, which was lying on the floor where he had left it. He walked over to the sideboard and put it in the drawer, on top of Mrs. Briggs's silly timetable.

"This stuff about the trucks going into the studio, that Mrs. Briggs goes on about, it really hasn't got anything to do with our petition, has it?" he said to his mom.

"No, but you shouldn't say these things."

"Why not, if it's true?"

"Because it's rude. You can hurt people's feelings by telling the truth too loud, you know."

"Oh," Mick said. So his mother was only pretending to agree with Mrs. Briggs.

He picked up the timetable, looked at it, then put it back in the drawer. He closed the drawer and turned away. Then something about the timetable struck him as odd.

He opened the drawer and looked again. It had a list of dates and times. There was something familiar about the dates. Then he realized what.

He got the newspaper page out of the drawer and looked at it again. "Blimey!" he said.

"Mind your language," his mom said. But he did not hear her. He held the two pieces of paper side by side.

"The dates are the same," he whispered.

"What are you talking about?" his mom said.

"Nothing," he replied.

"Then kindly talk about nothing in the kitchen. I'm watching the television."

Mick carried the two pieces of paper into the kitchen and sat down at the table to study them.

He had been right. Every day there had been a Disguise Gang raid, the trucks had annoyed Mrs. Briggs.

Now he knew what the men in the studio had been doing.

Kellerman's Studio was the Disguise Gang's hideout!

"Rubbish," Izzie said in a low voice.

"I can prove it," Mick replied.

They were standing side by side in assembly at school the following day. Their hymnbooks were open at "We Plough the Fields and Scatter," but their minds were elsewhere.

"Listen," Mick went on. "The dates of the Disguise Gang raids are the same as the dates on Mrs. Briggs's timetable."

"That doesn't prove anything," Izzie said more loudly. The eagle eye of Mr. Solomons rested on the pair.

"All good things around us are sent from Heaven above," Mick sang at the top of his voice. Mr. Solomons looked elsewhere.

Mick continued: "The gang get their disguises on, do the raid, and go back to the studio with the loot," he said. "The police think they use proper makeup and everything, don't they?"

Izzie looked less scornful then. They bowed their heads for the prayer, then started to file out of the hall.

Izzie said, "We ought to go to the police."

"You must be kidding!" Mick said.

"Why?"

"Well, suppose we're wrong? We'll get in trouble for trespassing in the studio."

Izzie thought for a minute. "We'll have to find proof," he said.

"How?"

"I dunno. There must be some way."

They sat down at their desks and got out their books.

CHAPTER FIVE

Izzie sat on his bike, holding onto the railings outside Mick's house, waiting for him to come out. He was puzzling over the problem of what to do about the Disguise Gang. There was no doubt about it: They needed proof that the men in the studio were the robbers. That much was easy enough to figure out. But how to get the proof?

Izzie wondered what would count as proof. If they could photograph the men changing out of their disguises, that would do. But they could not do that without getting caught.

Mick came out and slammed the door behind him. His bike was standing outside the house. He sat on the saddle, like Izzie, and leaned against the railings. "I think we ought to forget all about it," he said.

Izzie was amazed. "Why?"

"Well, why should we help get them caught?"

"Because—because they're thieves, that's why." To Izzie it seemed obvious.

"So? Why should we be on the side of the law? I'm on the side of the villains."

"Oh, don't be crazy, Mick. Besides, you'll never get a chance of adventure like this again. Just think—two schoolboys track down the notorious Disguise Gang, all on their own. We must try."

Mick thought for a moment. Izzie could see the struggle going on inside his friend. For Izzie, there were no two ways about it—if you could, you helped catch criminals. It seemed that Mick rather admired the criminals. But the lure of adventure was too much.

"But how to catch them, that's the problem," Mick said at last. Izzie knew that he had persuaded him now.

"I've been thinking about that," he replied. "The ideal thing would be to take photographs of them changing out of their disguises after they've done a raid."

"Yes, and get ourselves shot for our trouble," Mick said sarcastically.

"Hmm." Izzie frowned.

"Of course," Mick said, "we could photograph their disguises when they aren't there."

"Yes," Izzie said. "And their guns—and the stolen money, if there's any around."

"But we haven't got a camera."

"I have." Izzie was excited. This sounded like the answer.

"Can it take pictures indoors?"

"Yes. I've got a flash."

"Let's get it then."

They pushed themselves off the railings and rode away toward Izzie's house.

Izzie proudly showed Mick the camera. "It's a 35-mil," he said. Mick nodded. "This is the flash." Mick turned them over in his hands.

"Looks a bit complicated," he said.

"Yes. It's easy when you get used to it." He took it back and loaded the film. Then he packed the camera, the flash, and a box of bulbs into a leather case and slung it over his shoulder.

"It was my Christmas present," he said. "I was going to get a movie camera, but then the studio closed down and Father couldn't afford it."

They went downstairs and through the kitchen. Izzie said to his mother, "We're going to take some pictures. Do you mind if I miss dinner?"

"All right," she said. "But don't ask for egg and chips when you come in."

They cycled back to Canal Street and left the bikes at Mick's house. As they passed the studio entrance they saw that the night watchman was on duty, walking up the driveway with his German shepherd on a lead.

"We'll have to keep very quiet," Izzie told Mick.

They had to wait a few minutes at the canal bridge while some pedestrians passed by. Finally the street was clear, and they hopped over the parapet and clambered down the fence.

A light rain started to fall as they walked along the canal bank. There was a little more water in the narrow rivulet that ran through the mud, but their improvised stepping-stones were still there.

Izzie went first, his flashlight in his mouth and his camera across his back. As he crawled up the narrow tunnel, the concrete pipe seemed damper than usual to his touch. There also seemed to be a slight draft.

He had a notion that the draft meant something. It niggled at the back of his mind, but he could not quite remember what the explanation was.

He got to the manhole and shined his flashlight upward. Then he saw the explanation.

"That's funny," he said to Mick. "We must

have left the manhole cover off last time we were in here."

Mick grunted noncommittally and got into position for Izzie to climb on his shoulders. "I reckon I should go first next time," he said. "Give my shoulders a rest."

Izzie found the sides of the opening with his hands and took his weight off Mick's shoulders. Suddenly there was a blinding light. Strong hands grabbed his upper arms and heaved him out. A man's voice said, "Got you, you nosy little swine."

The light blinded Mick for a few seconds. He heard the voice and realized what it meant. It was a trap.

He dropped to his knees. They must have heard Izzie speak to him, so they knew he was there. He scuttled back down the pipe like a frightened rat. His hands and knees were bruised and grazed, but he did not notice. His heart pounded like a bass drum, and he kept falling over his hands.

He slowed up as he reached the end of the pipe. The men could not follow him down there, he realized—the pipe was too narrow. But would they be waiting at the end of it? He stopped. No, he decided. If they couldn't get down the pipe, they couldn't find out where it came out.

He poked his head out of the end. There seemed to be nobody around. He eased himself out and onto the first tire.

The rain was falling steadily now. Mick almost slipped on the wet rubber as he crossed the canal. He clambered up the opposite bank and made his way back to the road.

He was safe, but the gang had Izzie.

"What can I do?" Mick said to himself. He walked slowly back down the road toward his house. He certainly couldn't go in and have his tea as if nothing had happened. But he could not rescue Izzie all on his own.

He contemplated going to the police. He had no more doubts about whose side he was on. The gang had captured his friend, and that put Mick on the side of the law, temporarily at least. But what would the police do?

He did not know. But perhaps he ought to give them a chance.

Then he heard the truck. He looked up the driveway to the studio, and saw it coming toward the gate. He ran on past the gate to his house. Then he stopped.

Even if he went to the police, once the gang had left the studio there was no way Izzie could be traced.

Mick had to follow the truck.

He jumped on his bike. The truck pulled out of the studio entrance and turned away down the street. Mick pedaled after it. A guard was closing the studio gates as he passed.

Mick caught up with the truck as it waited at the white line to turn into the main road. He stayed with it as it crawled down Paul Street, which was narrow and had cars parked on either side. He lost it again on a clear stretch, but caught up at the traffic lights.

When it pulled away he stayed right behind it. It picked up speed along the two-lane highway. Mick pedaled furiously. His chest hurt now from the great gasping breaths he was taking. The rain drove into his face, and his sweater was soaking wet, yet underneath it he was sweating with the exertion.

The truck got about a hundred yards away from him, then pulled up at a traffic circle. Mick prayed for the traffic to keep it there a few moments longer. He was gaining on it rapidly when its brake lights flicked off and it shot forward into a gap in the line of cars. Mick piled on the pressure. Suddenly he realized he would have to stop at the traffic circle. He was going too fast. He jammed on his back brake, then the front. The wheels slid sideways on the wet pavement, the bike fell from under him, and Mick went headlong into the gutter.

CHAPTER SIX

Mick picked himself up off the road. He had banged his head and hurt his leg, but he seemed to be in one piece. A motorist had stopped and got out of his car.

"All right, son?" the man said.

"Yeah," Mick replied. "Thanks for stopping."

"You want to be more careful on these wet roads," the man said. He got back in his car and drove off.

Mick picked up his bike and wheeled it away on the pavement. He fought hard to stop himself crying. He had lost the truck for certain now.

The pain in his leg eased. He crossed the

road and mounted his bike. Then he pedaled slowly back toward Canal Street.

Once again he thought about the police. There seemed little point now. He would get into trouble for going in the studio, and they wouldn't be able to find Izzie anyway.

He wondered what the gang would do with Izzie. Perhaps they would make him swear to secrecy, then let him go.

No, they wouldn't be that dumb. Izzie might be stupid enough to keep his mouth shut if they made him promise, but they weren't likely to trust him.

He rode slowly up Canal Street and left his bike outside his house. He took off his wet shoes at the door to the apartment and carried them in.

His mom was sitting at the kitchen table, reading a book. Without looking up she said, "I hope you don't expect me to get your tea at this time of night."

"It's only seven o'clock," Mick muttered, but he had no stomach for an argument, or for his tea for that matter.

He dropped his shoes on the floor and went into the other room. His attempts at detecting had both turned out pretty badly, he thought. He got his clues out of the drawer—the ones he had picked up at Wheeler's house. He turned them over disconsolately. A fat lot of use they were. He put them back in the drawer. He felt useless himself. He had failed to trap the Disguise Gang. He turned away and switched the television set on.

Suddenly a bell rang in his mind. There was something odd about the words on the piece of paper he had picked up off Wheeler's garage floor. He went back to the drawer and took the clues out again.

He read the bank deposit slip carefully. It said: "National Westminster Bank, 25 Purley Street, Hinchley."

He had seen that address before. But where?

He racked his brains. Banks—why would he know anything about banks? Then he remembered.

He found the newspaper cutting about the Disguise Gang. Sure enough, they had raided the National Westminster Bank in Purley Street.

Coincidence, obviously. Then he looked at the date on the deposit slip. It was the day the bank had been raided. That was a bit too much of a coincidence.

But if it wasn't coincidence, what was it?

All it meant was that Mr. Norton Wheeler banked at the place that had been raided, and he had been there that day.

But if he had just been depositing some money, why had he taken the whole slip away with him? Unless . . .

Of course! That had to be it!

The Disguise Gang always posed as customers before they pounced. So one of the gang had been filling out a deposit slip while he watched for a chance to get behind the counter.

And the deposit slip had ended up on Mr. Norton Wheeler's garage floor.

Then Mick remembered where he had seen a brush like the one he had picked up when he found the deposit slip. There were several of them in the studio. They were makeup brushes.

Then it all fell into place. The guards at the studio always let the Disguise Gang's truck in. Why? They must have had instructions from the owner—Norton Wheeler.

Mr. Wheeler had to be the brains behind the Disguise Gang.

And now Mick knew where Izzie had been taken.

He put his shoes on again and dashed out of the apartment. His mother called out, "You're not going out again now, in this weather!" He ignored her and rushed down the stairs.

The rain had stopped now, but the roads

were still wet. However, Mick's thick tires were ideal for speeding along damp pavement. He would never have skidded at the traffic circle if he had not been in a panic.

He went along the route which the truck had taken, passing the spot where he had crashed. It took him five minutes to reach King Edward Avenue.

The truck was parked in Mr. Wheeler's driveway.

The lights were on in the house, because the gray sky and the rain had brought dusk early. Mick leaned his bike against the wall and looked over it into the garden.

He studied the place for a minute and then decided what he had to do.

He vaulted over the wall and crouched low in the flower bed. No one had seen him. He darted across a stretch of lawn and stopped again behind a rosebush. He made his way, under cover, to the very front of the house.

There was a narrow path all around the house. Mick got down on his hands and knees and crawled, keeping well below the level of the windows, until he reached the side of the house. Then he stood up, as there were no windows, and padded softly down to the back garden.

He surveyed the back of the house. If they

had brought Izzie here, where would they keep him?

Upstairs, obviously, so he couldn't escape through a window. And in a room that would lock.

There were three windows: one very wide one, one small one, and a third with frosted glass. The last would be the bathroom. And it had a light on.

He looked more closely at the bathroom window. The main pane of glass was frosted, but above it was a smaller pane of clear glass. The window was on the far corner of the house.

Below the window, at the side of the house, was a glass conservatory with a roof which sloped up to the house wall. Mick crawled across the back of the house to the conservatory.

He screwed up his nerve. Then he tiptoed down the side to the garbage cans, picked one up, and carried it back to the conservatory. He positioned it at the corner of the lean-to building, then climbed onto it.

From there it was a short jump to the roof. He pulled himself up and trod cautiously over the glass to the corner of the house. From there a pipe ran up, beside the bathroom window, to the gutter at the top. He got his fingers behind the pipe, took a tight grip, and swung his legs up.

Holding onto the pipe, he walked up the wall slowly. His arm muscles ached, but he knew he could do it—he had done similar things in the school gym.

He inched up beside the bathroom window until his face was level with the upper, clear pane of glass. Then he looked inside.

Izzie stared into the face of the man who had lifted him clear of the manhole. "So you're the little mouse who's been nosing around in here, are you?" the man said. He had heavy black eyebrows and a thick moustache which followed the corners of his mouth. He held Izzie's face close to his own as he spoke. His breath smelled bad.

Izzie was too shocked and frightened to speak. He just stared, white-faced, at his captor. The man's powerful hands set him down on the floor, turned him around, and twisted one arm behind his back. "Move," he said.

He pushed Izzie through the door, across the corridor, and into Studio B. Up to that point, Izzie had cherished a faint hope that the man might just be one of the night watchmen. But as he entered Studio B that hope died.

There were two other men in there. One of them was bent over, putting on a shoe, when Izzie walked in, and Izzie could see a familiar bald spot on the top of the man's head.

It was the Disguise Gang.

Izzie's captor said, "Look what I found, Gus."

The man with the bald spot looked up. "A sneaking kid," he said.

Izzie looked at the third man. He had bright red hair and freckles. He looked at Izzie for a moment, then put his hand to his head. He pulled off a wig, and Izzie saw short gray hair underneath it. The man said, "What do we do about that?"

"I dunno," Gus replied.

The man holding Izzie twisted his arm a little more. "Little runt could ruin everything," he said. There was a nasty note in his voice.

Izzie said, "You're hurting my arm."

"Shut up, or I'll hurt your head."

"Ease off, Jerry," said Gus. The man released the pressure on Izzie's arm.

Gus said, "Come here, son." Jerry let go of his arm and Izzie walked across to Gus.

"What were you doing here?" Gus asked.

"Just playing," Izzie said. "We played with the costumes and the props and everything. If you go, I won't tell anyone about you, I promise."

"What do you mean, tell anyone about us?"

said Jerry. "What is there to tell? We've got a right to be here. You're the trespasser. Who would be interested in us?"

"I mean, I won't go to the police or anything—if you'll just let me go," Izzie blurted out. He was near to tears now.

"Go to the police?" said the man who had taken off the red wig.

"Don't bother, Alec," said Gus. "He knows. It's obvious."

Izzie realized how stupid he had been. The gang had not been sure whether he understood what they were doing in the studio. Now, he had let it out that he suspected them of doing something illegal. If he had played dumb they might have let him go.

The man called Alec went to the sink and washed off his freckles. As he dried his face with a towel he said, "So, what do we do with him? He certainly can't be let loose."

"Have to take him to the boss," Gus said. "Otherwise, whatever I do will be wrong." He put on his other shoe and shrugged into a coat. Meanwhile the other two packed away the clothes, wigs, and makeup gear that were lying around and put them in a cupboard.

"All right, kid," said Jerry when they were ready. "You're coming for a ride." He took Izzie's arm again and pushed him out through the door. Alec shined a flashlight, and the four of them walked down the long corridor.

They came around to the front of the studio. Through the wide glass doors Izzie could see a van. They went outside, Gus locking the studio door behind him.

Jerry pushed Izzie forward to the rear door of the van, and fished in his pocket for a key. As he turned the key in the lock, Izzie seized his chance. He wrenched his arm away from Jerry's grip and dashed away.

Jerry gave a shout. Gus turned away from the studio door and saw Izzie running past him. He stuck out a foot and Izzie tripped over it, falling full length on the gravel.

He lay there for a moment, full of despair. His face was cut and grazed by the gravel, and his legs felt bruised where he had cannoned into Gus's foot. He could not hold back the tears any longer.

Jerry hauled him to his feet and slapped his face once. Izzie yelped with pain.

"Take it easy, Jerry," said Alec in a low voice. "He's only a kid."

"What do you want me to do, give him a medal?" Jerry replied. "I'm going to teach him a lesson."

Gus cut in: "Just put him in the back of the van and keep an eye on him, Jerry."

Izzie was thrown roughly into the van where he lay, face down. Jerry got into the back with him, and the other two got into the front. Izzie heard the engine start up, and the van roared down the driveway.

Izzie had no idea where the van went. He lay on the hard metal floor and tried to ease the pressure off his bruises. After what seemed like a very long journey, the vehicle stopped.

Gus said, "Better blindfold the kid, so he doesn't know where he is."

Jerry found an oily rag on the van floor and tied it tightly around Izzie's eyes. Then he lifted the boy out of the van and set him down. Once again, he twisted his arm and pushed him forward.

Izzie could feel a hard surface under his feet. After a moment Jerry said, "Up the step," and Izzie stumbled up a step. He could tell then that he was indoors.

A new voice said, "What on earth is this?" The voice sounded older and less coarse than those of the three crooks.

Izzie heard Gus say, "Kid we caught nosing around the studio, boss. He said he wouldn't go to the police if we set him free."

"You fools, why did you bring him here?"

"Didn't know what else to do," Gus's voice came back.

"Damn." There was a silence for a minute.

Then the boss said, "Well, let's get him out of the way while I think about it. Take him upstairs and tie him up."

Jerry said, "This way, kid." He steered Izzie up a staircase and into a room. Then Izzie was pushed down on a hard seat, and his hands and ankles were bound tightly. Finally the door shut and footsteps descended the stairs.

CHAPTER SEVEN

Izzie contemplated his plight miserably. He knew too much about the Disguise Gang, and they knew he knew. He understood the problem they were now discussing. It was how to shut him up. And he could think of only one way—kill him.

It followed that he had nothing to lose by trying to escape, he decided. That bucked him up a bit, and he started to explore his surroundings. With his bound hands he felt the seat he was sitting on and discovered it was a lavatory. They must have locked me in the bathroom, he thought.

He flexed his muscles, and found that his bonds were not very tight. He wriggled his hands back and forth. He seemed to be getting somewhere. After a while he stopped to rest his aching wrists. Then he tried again.

Suddenly he heard a tap on the window. He turned his face toward it, but of course the movement was useless, for he still had his blindfold on. The tapping stopped. Izzie puzzled over it for a moment, then decided it was just one of those mysterious noises houses make from time to time.

He struggled with his bonds again, and suddenly his wrists were free. He whipped off the blindfold and looked around him. He was in a large bathroom. On the far side of the room was the bath, and between that and where Izzie sat was the door. Opposite the door was a shower and the window.

As Izzie untied the cords around his ankles, a plan started to take shape in his mind. The handle was on the far side of the door, so that you had to come right into the room to see the toilet on which Izzie was sitting.

On a shelf beside the washbasin was a cluster of bottles and jars. Izzie chose a large, heavy bottle of after-shave. He smelled it and recognized the smell as the one he had noticed when the boss had been nearby.

He heard footsteps on the stairs. He picked up the bottle, then climbed on the back end of the bath, pressing himself against the wall.

He put his head right back and held his

breath, praying that whoever came through the door would not see him until it was too late.

The key turned in the lock and the door opened. Izzie's hand, clutching the heavy bottle, was above his head. Jerry walked in.

Izzie brought the bottle down on the man's head with all his might. It smashed, sending bits of glass and a shower of scent all over the place. Jerry slumped to the floor with a thud. Izzie sprang down from his position and went through the bathroom door.

He found himself at the top of the stairs. Straight ahead of him was a landing, and the stairs ran down alongside it.

He heard a voice from downstairs saying, "What was that bump?"

Another voice said, "Have a look."

Izzie was halfway down the stairs when a door opened and Alec came out. He saw Izzie and started toward him.

Izzie turned and fled back up the stairs. Alec chased after him, taking the stairs three at a time.

Izzie turned at the top and ran along the landing a couple of yards. Alec got to the top of the stairs. Izzie vaulted the rail and landed nimbly halfway down the stairs.

Then Gus was at the bottom. "Damn kid!" he roared. Izzie was still holding the end of the broken bottle. He rushed at Gus and hurled the

jagged glass at the man's face. Gus jumped out of the way, stumbled and fell.

Izzie jumped over his body and raced for the front door. Alec pounded down the stairs after him. He heard the boss's voice say, "Grab him, quick, you blundering idiots!"

Izzie had the front door unlatched when Alec's hand landed on his shoulder. Alec yanked him back from the door just as he pulled it open.

"Got you, you horrible little swine," Alec said.

The door swung open and Izzie saw, on the doorstep, the tall figures of his father and a burly policeman. The policeman's hand was raised as if about to knock on the door.

Alec squealed and let go of Izzie.

"Don't bother to run for it," the policeman said. "The house is surrounded."

Izzie looked back down the hall to see the boss reach into his pocket. Suddenly the policeman shot past Izzie, moving incredibly quickly for such a big man. The boss had a pistol halfway out of his pocket when the policeman's fist floored him. Izzie dashed into his father's arms.

Another policeman entered the hall, and suddenly the place seemed to be full of them. Alec and Gus surrendered meekly. Handcuffs were clapped on them, and they were led out. Gus touched his hands to the gash on his forehead, and glared evilly at Izzie as he passed him and was led to the waiting police van.

"Did you do that to him?" Izzie's father asked.

"Yes," Izzie said, not sure whether to be proud or ashamed.

A policeman called from upstairs: "There's another one here, Sarge—out cold."

Mr. Izard looked at Izzie and raised his eyebrows.

Izzie nodded. "I did that, too," he said. "Are you mad at me?"

His father looked at him for a minute. Then he ruffled his hair. "Of course not, silly," he said, a bit hoarsely. "I'm proud of you."

"How did you find me?" Izzie asked.

"It was Mick," answered Mr. Izard. "He figured out where you were—how he managed it I'm not quite sure. He came along and saw you through a window."

"Yes," Izzie said. "It must have been him who tapped on the glass."

"Anyway, then he came to me and told me everything and I got the police. Mick led us around here. He's out there now, in one of the police cars."

Izzie left his father and ran out to find Mick.

Much later, Izzie and his father drove Mick home from the police station. Mr. Izard said,

"There's a piece of good news for you to tell your mother, Mick. I've managed to raise the money to get the studio going again."

"Great," said Mick. "And with Norton Wheeler in jail for being the boss of the Disguise Gang . . ."

"Your house won't be knocked down after all!" Izzie finished.

"Blimey," said Mick. "What a lucky day."

About the Author

KEN FOLLETT is the author of many international best sellers, including *Eye of the Needle*, *On Wings of Eagles*, and *Pillars of the Earth*. He lives in London with his wife and children.

Look for another
Ken Follett adventure
available in Apple Paperback:

THE POWER TWINS

Fritz and Helen looked at one another. Helen said, "I think we both would like to help solve the dispute in outer space, but we're just not sure we can do the job."

"Let me worry about that," said Uncle Grigorian. "I've found out a lot about you in the last few months. I know you're clever and fair-minded. Besides, I'm going to give you some help, which I can't tell you about until I'm sure you agree to go."

They looked at one another again. Then they both said, "We'll go." Fritz added, "Tell us what help we'll get."

"I'm going to give you the Powers," he said.